The Monkey and the Bee

Come On! Play Ball!

Eddie's Moving Day

Peek-a-Boo

the read-it-yourself storybook

the read-it-yourself storybook

Edited by
Leland B. Jacobs, Professor of Education
Teachers College, Columbia University

A GOLDEN BOOK • NEW YORK
Western Publishing Company, Inc.,
Racine, Wisconsin 53404

Contents

Printed in the U.S.A. GOLDEN®, GOLDEN & DESIGN®, and A GOLDEN BOOK® are trademarks of Western Publishing Company, Inc. Library of Congress Catalog Card Number: 77-154823 ISBN 0-307-16824-7

MCMXCII

Foreword

One of the young child's most spectacular accomplishments is learning to read. It is almost like magic that, somehow, what have been little squizzly black marks on a page become words that can be recognized and pronounced, and can produce meanings.

Of course, the child has been getting ready for this to happen in many ways. He has been noticing forms in his toys. He has been putting shapes together with blocks or with his mother's saucepans. He has heard stories read. He has been seeing what pictures and television have to tell him. He has been observing signs on highways and billboards and store windows. And he knows that color, design, and print help him know which cereal box is which in the cupboard at home.

But then the moment of reading comes, when he can tell what the little marks say and respond to what they mean to him. When that moment comes, he needs materials to read that he can enjoy as well as comprehend. For enjoyment in reading is one of the chief keys to success in reading. What one enjoys he is likely to turn to again and again.

Because the young child is not able to recognize great numbers of words in print, he must have things to read that are enjoyable while not overtaxing his ability to unlock the words on the page. This means that the reading material must be lively enough to sustain his interest while easy enough in vocabulary to keep his feeling of accomplishment high. The young reader, too, wants variety in what he reads: stories that tickle his funny bone, that extend his imagination, that move along with well-paced action, that give a lilting sound effect when read aloud. In other words, the child's early reading material must say something to him that he takes pleasure in having said, in words and in sentence length that he can manage without too much reading difficulty. And the pictures are important, too, for giving him clues to what will be on the page.

The stories in this collection are the kinds of "read-it-yourself" material that surely will appeal to the beginning reader. They are lively, fun-filled, and provide such a variety of plots and story forms that monotony is avoided. Thus the child will be challenged to go on to the next story, and the next, with each a little more difficult—but not too much so—than the previous one.

As a child moves from greater dependency toward increasing independence, in all aspects of his development, he lets adults know, in one way or another, that he wants to do it himself. He wants to prove to himself, and to older folks whom he respects, that he is on his way toward being quite able to cope with the task at hand. So it is with the beginning reader. And when he has story material that encourages his independence, how he takes to it. For as he reads, page after page, story after story, he is telling everyone who will listen, "I can read!"

Leland B. Jacobs

The Monkey and the Bee

Story by Leland B. Jacobs
Pictures by Kelly Oechsli

See! See!
What do I see?

I see a tree.

Yes, I see a tree.

See! See!
What do I see?

I see a bee.

Yes, I see a bee.

See! See!
What do you see?

I see a monkey.
I see a tree.

Do you see a bee?
Oh! Oh!

I see a monkey.
I see a tree.

Do you see a bee?

Oh! Oh!

A tree?

A bee?

I see the monkey
in the tree.

What do you see?

Yes, what do you see?

Look! Look!
What do you see?

I see the bee
fly to the tree.

I see the bee
on the monkey's tree.

Look in the tree.

What do you see?

I see the monkey
look at the bee.

Oh!

See!

What do you see?

I see the monkey
hit at the bee.
Oh, the monkey
hits at the bee.

Look! Look!
Look at the bee.

The bee bit the monkey
on the knee.

Look at the monkey.
Look at the bee.

Oh, me! Oh, me!

Hit.

Bit.

Bit.

Hit.

The bee bit the monkey.
The monkey hit at the bee.

The monkey hit
at the bee.
Oh, me!
The monkey hit the tree!

Look! Look!

Do you see the bee?

Yes, I see the bee.

The bee flies from the tree.

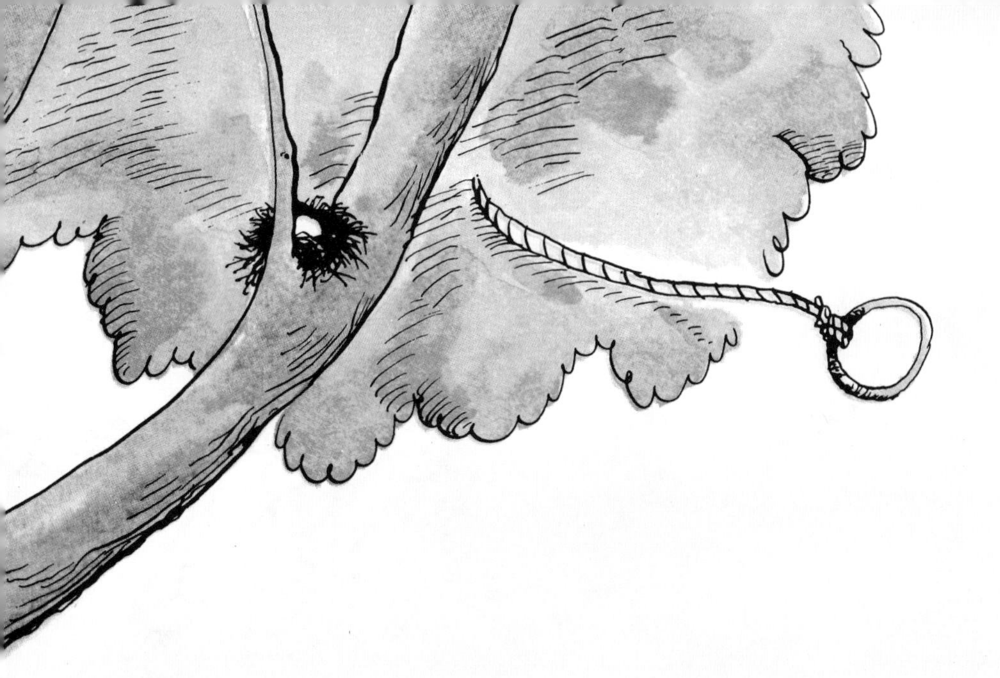

The bee flies at me!

See!

Oh! Oh!

The bee flies at ME!

Tony and His Friends

Story and pictures by
Ken Wagner

Tony lived in a zoo.

Tony was a lion.

He was a friendly lion.

“I need some hair for a nest,”
said a bird.
“Take all you want,” said Tony.

"I need some hair, too,"
said another bird.
"Take all you want," said Tony.

"We want hair, too,"
said more birds.
"Take all you want," said Tony.

“Make nice nests,”
Tony said to the birds.

"Look at the funny lion,"
said a man.
"He has no hair."
But Tony said,
"I have one hair."

"A lion with no hair!"
said the zoo keeper.
"You look funny."

"I wanted to help the birds,"
said Tony.

"I can hide like this,"
said Tony.

"No, no, no,"
said the zoo keeper.

"I can wear a hat,"
said Tony.
"No, no, no,"
said the zoo keeper.

"I can use my tail,"
said Tony.
"No, no, no,"
said the zoo keeper.

A man told Mr. Harry about Tony.
"Go to the zoo," said the man.
"Look at the funny lion
with no hair."

Mr. Harry went to the zoo.
He said to the zoo keeper,
"I grow hair.
I will help Tony the lion."

"Does this feel good?"
asked Mr. Harry.
"Yes," said Tony.

“Can you feel anything?”
asked Mr. Harry.
“Yes, yes,” said Tony.

Tony's one hair began
to grow,
and grow,

and grow.

"My, my, my,"
said the zoo keeper.

“You need a haircut,”
the zoo keeper said to Tony.

"Why are you sad?"
asked a bird.
"I look funny," said Tony.

"We will help you,"
said the birds.
And they did.

"Look at the funny lion,"
said a man.
"He looks nice,"
said another man.

"I will wear this
till my own hair
grows back,"
said Tony.
And he did.

Emily's Moo

Story and pictures by *Tibor Gergely*

Emily was a little cow.
She lived in a field.

Emily could eat grass.

She could smell the flowers.

She could dance
under the moon.

But Emily was not happy,
for she could not moo.

"Maybe I eat the wrong things,"
said Emily.
So she ate berries.

She ate flowers.

She ate leaves.

But still she could not moo.

She said to Goat,
"Please show me
how to moo."

Goat made a sound.
But it was a goat's sound.
Emily said,
"That is not a moo."

She said to Dog,
"Please show me
how to moo."

Dog said, "Woof, woof."
But it was a dog's sound.
Emily said,
"That is not a moo."

Emily went to Rooster.
She said,
"Please show me
how to moo."

Rooster said,
"Cock-a-doodle-doo."
But it was a rooster's sound.
Emily said,
"That is not a moo."

Emily began to cry.

Brown Cow said,
"Why are you crying, Emily?"

Emily said,
"I am a cow.
But I cannot moo."

"Oh, come now,"
said Brown Cow.
"All cows can moo.
You can moo, too.
I will show you how."

"Open your mouth, like this,"
said Brown Cow.
"Let the sound come out,
like this—moo.
That is how a cow moos."

"Now you try it,"
she said to Emily.

Emily opened her mouth.
Out came a sound.
It was not a goat's sound.
It was not a dog's sound.
It was not a rooster's sound.

It was a big, big "MOO."

Goat came running.
Dog came running.
Rooster came running.

They all said,
"Good for Emily!
She did it!
She did it!"

Now Emily moos.
She moos all day long.
And she moos
as she dances
under the yellow moon.

Come On! Play Ball!

Story and pictures by
Ilse-Margret Vogel

I am small,

You are tall.

Come on!
Play ball
in the hall.

I like the hall
for playing ball.

Look out.
The ball
will hit
the wall.

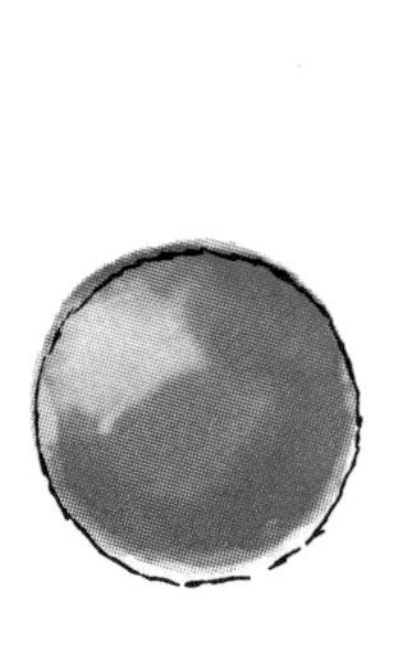

Run and catch it.
It will fall.

I will not let
the red ball fall.

I see a Tiger
in the hall.

A Tiger
is
sleeping
by the wall.

Look at me.
I catch the ball.

Now I throw.
I throw up high.

You throw too high,
too high, too high.

It is too small
inside our hall.
Too small
for running
and
playing ball!

Go out! Go out!
The big blue sky
is very good
for throwing high.

I see a bee
and butterfly.
But I do not see
our ball up high.

I see
the clouds and sun.
But I
do not see our ball
up high.

ANIMAL
APARTMENTS
LETTERS

I throw again.
I throw it high.
I throw the ball
high in the sky.

Hippo!
Did you see our ball?

It went up.
But it did not fall.
It went up
very, very high.
High up
in the big, blue sky!

I did not see
your sky-high ball.
I did not see
your ball at all!

I do not fly
up in the sky.
I stay down on the ground.
Good-by.

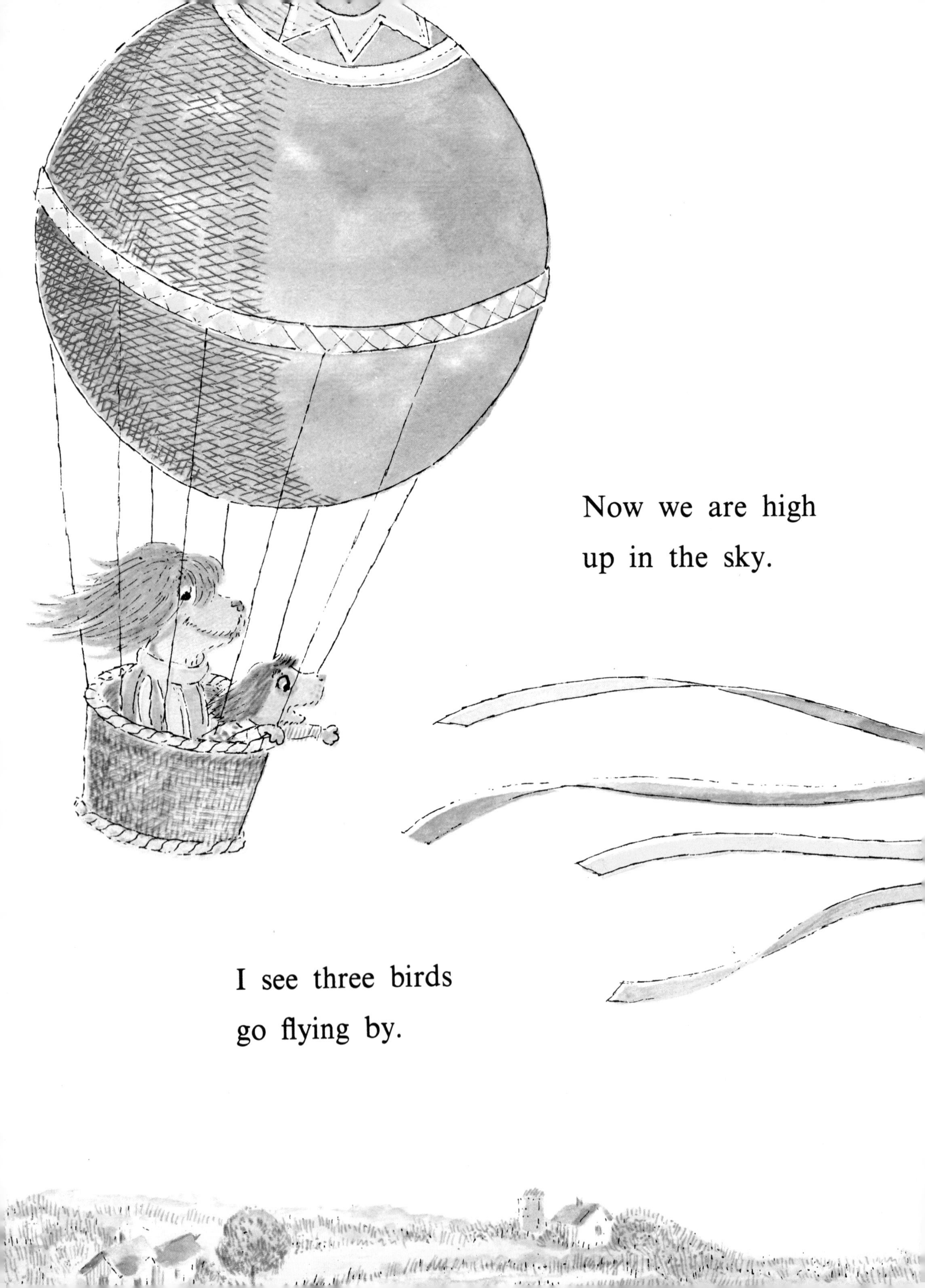

Now we are high
up in the sky.

I see three birds
go flying by.

One bird is thin.

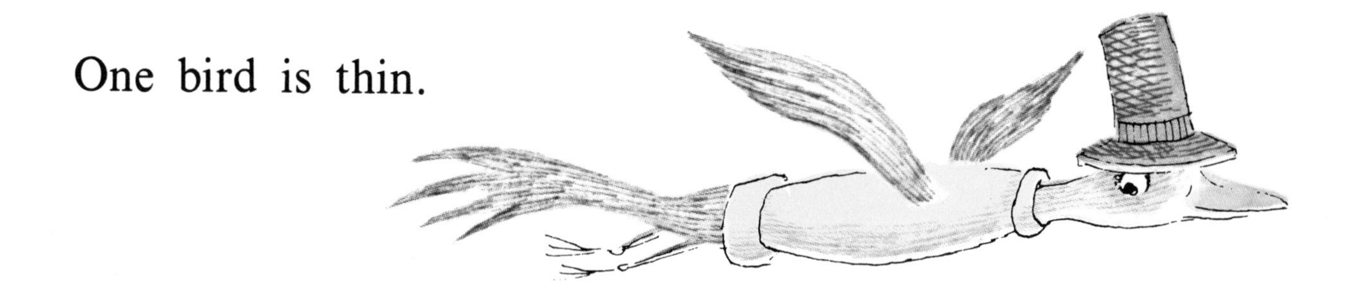

One bird is fat.

One has ribbons on her hat.

But I do not see
the ball we tossed.
Can it be
our ball is lost?

I see you.
Do you see me?

Owl, we see you
in the tree.
Did you see
the ball we tossed?
We tossed it high.
Now it is lost.

Your big balloon
is all I see.
It looks like
a big red ball to me.

Donkey!

Did you see our ball?

It went up high.

It did not fall.

Yes, yes, yes.
I saw your ball.
I saw it fall
by that red wall.

Many balls
go over walls.
Red and green
and yellow balls!
Blue and white
and purple balls!

But most of them
stay on the ground.
They do not move
till they are found.

Look!

I have the ball we tossed.

Our ball is found.

It is not lost.

Now I say
to one and all,
"Come on!
Come on!
Come on!
Play ball!"

Peek-a-Boo

Story and pictures by
Ilse-Margret Vogel

You and I
play
peek-a-boo!

Let me play too!

Peek-a-boo!
I see you!

I see you
in that old shoe.

Do you see me
behind the tree?

We need some glue
to fix the shoe!

What shall I do?
I shall paint
the shoe blue!

GLUE

Shoo! Shoo! Shoo!
I play in that shoe.
Do not paint
my old shoe blue.
And do not fix
the toe with glue.
I like fresh air
in my old shoe!

See! A kite
is going by!

I will go
up in the sky!

Now it is up, up, up
we go.
Up in the air
with our friend Crow!

This kite
is nice and wide.
And I shall hide
on the other side.

A cloud is good
for hiding too,
in the game
of peek-a-boo!

Peek-a-boo,
Pretty Cow!

Pretty Cow
sees us now!

I see mice!
Yes I do!
Peek-a-boo!
Moo, moo, moo!

Hello,

Mother Kangaroo!

Will you play

some peek-a-boo?

Mice, I have
no time today.
But Little Kangaroo
will play.

Peek-a-boo!
I see you!

See the Lion
by the sea?
He likes to play
with you and me!

I know you mice
like peek-a-boo.
But I am having
my shampoo.
I have no time
to play with you!

The moon is up
above the town.
But this nice kite
is going down.

Then down is where
we have to go.
And peek-a-boo
to all below.

Bear, your kite
is full of mice!

Yes, I know!
but mice
are nice.

Good-by, Dog.
Good-by, Crow.
Good-by, Bear.
We have to go.
It is late
and time to go.

Come to supper.
I have stew.

Peek-a-boo!

We love you!

I love you, too!

It is too late
for peek-a-boo.
Now is the time
for supper stew!
Then into bed
with both of you!

MOVING

Eddie's Moving Day

by ***Janet Deering***
Pictures by ***Joe Kaufman***

One day Eddie's mother said,
"Eddie, your father has a new job.
We are going to move."

Eddie was happy where he was.
He liked his house,
and his yard,
and his apple tree.
He liked his friends.
Most of all, he liked Elmer.

Elmer was Eddie's trick turtle.
Elmer could carry sticks.
He could stand on his hind legs.
He could hide in his shell.

Eddie and Elmer and Eddie's friends
played in Eddie's house.
They played in Eddie's yard.
They climbed Eddie's apple tree.
"I think I will stay here,"
Eddie said to his mother.

"We'd be lonesome without you, Eddie,"
his mother said.
"I hate to leave this house,"
said Eddie.
"Can we take it with us?"
"No, Eddie," his mother said.
"It must stay with the yard
and the apple tree."

"Well, I hate to leave my friends,"
said Eddie.
"Can we take them with us?"
"No, Eddie," his mother said.
"They must stay
with their mothers and fathers."

"Well, can Elmer come along with us?"
said Eddie.
"Yes, Eddie," his mother said.
That made Eddie happy.
He would not be so lonesome
with Elmer and his tricks.

A moving van drove up
in front of Eddie's house.
"The moving men are here," said Eddie.
Everyone was busy.
Everyone was in a hurry.
Everyone said,
"Stay out of the way, Eddie."

Eddie and Elmer stayed out of the way.

They sat in the apple tree.

They watched everyone being busy.

By and by it was time to go.

Eddie put Elmer by the apple tree.

"Stay there, Elmer," said Eddie.

"I will say good-bye."

“Good-bye, house,” said Eddie.
“Good-bye, yard and apple tree.
You will always be
my favorite house,
and my favorite yard,
and my favorite apple tree.”

Eddie's friends were there.
"Good-bye, everyone," said Eddie.
"You will always be
my favorite friends."

"We must go now,"
Eddie's father said.
"Hurry, Eddie!" said his mother.
"Wait for Elmer and me,"
said Eddie.

Eddie ran to the apple tree.

Elmer was not there.

"Where is Elmer?" everyone said.

They all looked by the apple tree.
They looked and looked.
"Elmer has run away," Eddie said.
"Elmer does not want to move away.
Elmer! Elmer! Come back!"

"We must go," Eddie's father said.
"Your friends will look for Elmer.
They will take care of him."
"Good-bye," Eddie's friends said.
"We will look for Elmer
and take care of him."

"Good-bye, Eddie," said the moving men.
"We will see you soon."
"Good-bye, everyone," Eddie said.
"And good-bye, Elmer,
wherever you are."
Eddie was very sad.

They drove,
and drove,
and drove.
Eddie was lonesome for Elmer.

They drove and drove some more.

Eddie was even more lonesome for Elmer.

By and by they drove up
in front of the new house.
"We must get ready for the moving men,"
Eddie's father said.

Eddie looked at the new house.
It looked very much like the house
he had left behind.

Eddie looked at the new yard.
It looked very much like the yard
he had left behind.

There was even a tree
that looked like his favorite tree.
"I wish Elmer were here," Eddie said.
"Then I would be happy."

Soon Eddie saw someone looking at him,
and then another someone,
and still another someone.
"Hi," said Eddie.
No one said "hi" back.
Eddie climbed his new tree
and looked at the new girls and boys.
They looked very much like the friends
he had left behind.

By and by the moving men drove up.
"Hi," Eddie said to the moving men.
"Hi, Eddie," said the moving men.
"We have a surprise for you!"

The new boys and girls
came to see the surprise.
"Hi!" they said to Eddie.
"Where is the surprise?"
The surprise was Elmer.
The moving men had found him.

"Elmer does tricks!"
Eddie said to his new friends.
They watched Elmer.
They watched him carry sticks.
They watched him stand
on his hind legs.

“This is a good place, Elmer,”
Eddie said.
“We are going to like it here!”

Too Many Bozos

by Lilian Moore
pictures by Susan Perl

"Mother," said Danny Drake.
"May I have a dog?"

Danny's mother looked at Danny.

"Danny Drake," she said.
"You asked me that last week.
And what did I say?"

"No," said Danny.

"You asked me that the week before,"
said his mother.
"And what did I say?"

"No," said Danny.

Danny's mother said, "No!
I'm sorry, Danny.
Our house is too small for a dog."

"But I have a good name for a dog,"
said Danny.
"I want to call him Bozo."

"NO, Danny!" said his mother.
And Danny knew it was time to stop.

Danny ran out to the park to play. He played in the park all morning with his friend, Pete.

They played they were pirates on a pirate ship.

The little brook in the park
was a great river.
Up and down the river
went the pirates in their ship.

Danny saw the little frog first.
He knew at once he wanted
that frog for a pet.

Pete helped him catch it.

They found a box and put the frog in it.

Then Danny carried the frog home.

"Oh, boy!" Danny said to the frog.
"Am I glad I found you.
Won't Mom be surprised!"

Mom *was* surprised.

Danny held up the frog.

"Now I have a pet," he told his mother.
"Do you want to hold him?"

"No, thanks," said Danny's mother.

"I'm going to call my pet Bozo,"
Danny said. "Bozo the Frog."

"Please tell Bozo the Frog to stay
in *your* room," said Danny's mother.

Danny kept Bozo the Frog in his room
and took good care of him.

He made a nice home for him
and gave him bits of meat to eat.

What fun the frog was!

And what a good jumper!

First Danny put down one book.

Bozo jumped right over it.

Danny put down two books, then three.

And Bozo jumped over them all!

One day Bozo made one jump too many. The door to his house was open.

Jump! Bozo was out of his house.

Jump! Jump! He was out of Danny's room.

Jump! Jump! Jump! He was here and there, all over the house.

At last Bozo found the best place of all.
It was a place with water,
so he jumped right in it.

He was in the kitchen sink.
The sink was full of dishes.
Bozo sat on Mother's best green dish.

Danny's mother came in to do the dishes.

She screamed when she saw Bozo.

Bozo was so scared he jumped
out of the sink, right at Danny's mother!

"A frog in my sink! Ugh!" cried his mother.
"Danny take that frog
out of the house at once!"

Sadly, Danny put Bozo into the box and walked back to the park.

On the way he met his friend Billy.

"Look what I have!" said Billy.
He held up a little cage.

"Look what I have!" said Danny.
He opened the box a little.

Right then and there—they swapped!
Billy took the box and Danny took the cage.

Danny ran all the way home.
"Oh, boy!" he said to himself.
"Am I glad I met Billy.
Won't Mom be surprised!"

Mom *was* surprised.

Danny held up the cage for her to see. There was a little white mouse in it.

"This is my new pet," Danny said. "I'm going to call him Bozo. Bozo the Mouse."

Danny took the mouse out
and let him hang onto his sweater.

"Look, Mom!" he cried.
"See what Bozo does!
Do you want to try it?"

"No, thanks," said Danny's mother.
"And Danny Drake, don't let that mouse
out of your room!"

"It's all right, Mom," said Danny.
"Bozo the Mouse won't get in the sink."

Danny took good care of Bozo the Mouse.
He cleaned Bozo's cage.
He put food and water in it.
He played with Bozo every day.

Bozo the Mouse did not get into the sink.

But one morning he got out of his cage.

He got out of Danny's room.
And he went down to the kitchen.

Sniff! Sniff! went Bozo the Mouse.

The kitchen was full of a good smell.
Danny's mother had just made a cake
for the Big Cake Sale.

That is, it *was* for the Cake Sale
until Bozo the Mouse saw it.
Bozo the Mouse liked the cake very much.

When Danny's mother took a good look at her cake, she cried, "My cake! Oh, my lovely, lovely cake!"

Then she said, "Danny Drake, take that cake-eating mouse out of the house at once!"

Sadly, Danny put Bozo the Mouse into his cage.

"The best place to take Bozo the Mouse," thought Danny, "is back to the pet shop. That's where Billy got his white mouse in the first place."

So Danny took Bozo to the pet shop. The pet shop man was glad to get the white mouse back.

Danny and the pet shop man made a swap.

Danny ran all the way home.

"Oh, boy!" he said to himself. "Am I glad I went to the pet shop! I wonder what Mom will say when she sees what I have now."

Danny's mother did not say anything at first. She just looked at the box Danny was holding.

"What in the world is that?" she asked.

Danny held up the box.

"This is an ant farm," Danny told her.

"See all those ants?

I can watch them work and everything."

"Ants!" cried Danny's mother,

"I can just see ants all over the house.

No ants, Danny Drake!

And I mean it!"

"Mother," said Danny Drake at last.
"I just *have* to have some kind of pet."

"Yes," said Danny's mother.
"I can see that you do!"

She put her arm around Danny.

"I know just the pet for you," she said.

"Is it better than a frog?" asked Danny.

"Much better," said his mother.

"Is it better than a white mouse?"

"Much, much better," said his mother.

"Is it better than an ant farm?"

"Oh, yes!" said his mother.
"Much, much, much better!"

"Danny Drake," she said.
"How would you like a dog?"

"A DOG!" cried Danny. "A DOG!"

"A little dog," said Danny's mother,
"because our house is little.
But a real dog."

"Oh, boy!" said Danny, "A dog!
And guess what I'm going to call him."

"Bozo," said Danny. "Bozo the Dog."

"Bozo!" said Danny's mother.
"What a surprise!"

Tony and
His Friends

Too Many Bozos

EMILY'S MOO